D1515921

Published by Brown Watson (Leicester) Ltd.

© 1986 Rand McNally & Company
Printed and bound in the German Democratic Republic

THE CHRISTMAS SNOWMAN

by Diane Sherman
Illustrated by Sharon Kane

Brown Watson

ENGLAND

SAMMY was a handsome new
snowman. He had button eyes, a
carrot nose, and a bowler hat. But
Sammy didn't want to be an ordinary
snowman. He wanted to be a
Christmas snowman.

"A *Christmas* snowman?" said
Squeaky Squirrel, as he jumped off
a branch to say hello. "Now that
would be something special."

"*Very* special," said Corky Crow. He swooped low, and landed on Sammy's shoulder. "But how can you be a Christmas snowman?"

"Well," said Sammy, "first I'll need some decorations. You do lots of travelling, Crow. Have you seen something I can use?"

Corky Crow thought a minute,
then took off for his favourite spot,
the dump. On a pile of rubbish he saw
a wreath that looked like new.
Carrying it back in his beak, he
dropped it over Sammy's head.

"Thank you," said Sammy. "This looks fine around my neck. Now what about you, Squirrel? Do you have anything I can use?"

Squeaky Squirrel thought for a minute, then scurried back to his hidey-hole in the tree. From deep inside he pulled out a big red bow he'd found on the ground.

"Here you are, Snowman," he
said. He tucked the ribbon on
Sammy's hat.

Fanny Field Mouse heard the
commotion and poked her nose out
from under a log. "A new snowman!
How do you do!"

"He wants to be a *Christmas* snowman," said Squeaky. "Do you have any decorations we can use?"

Fanny thought a minute. Then
she disappeared in her hole. Soon
she was back with her children behind
her, pushing a huge gold ball.

"It's a tree ornament," said
Fanny. "The children found it last
year."

"Beautiful," said Sammy, as they fastened it on his chest. "Thank you, friends. Do I look like a Christmas snowman now?"

"Oh, yes," shouted Squeaky Squirrel. "Seeing you makes me feel all happy and Christmas-y inside." He clapped his paws together and started doing somersaults.

The Field Mouse children began tumbling, too.

Sammy smiled as he watched. He liked making everyone happy.

"*I* feel like dancing," Fanny said. She glided around the others. "There's just one thing. Christmas is for everyone. The animals can see you here, but not many people will."

Sammy thought about it. Then
he had an idea. "Come here, Corky
Crow," he said. He whispered into
Corky's ear.

With a flap and a flutter of his wings, Corky flew off. He found some children racing downhill on their sledges. Swooping low, he grabbed a mitten someone left on the ground.

"Come back, Crow," the children yelled. They grabbed their sledges and followed to where the snowman stood.

"Someone decorated the snowman!" They stood admiring Sammy.
"Doesn't he make you feel good?"

said the children. "A real Christmas snowman !" Joining hands, they danced all around Sammy.

Up in the tree, Corky Crow
danced too, clapping his wings to
keep time. Squeaky Squirrel drummed
on a branch with some twigs. And
down below, behind a log, the Field
Mouse children frolicked.

At night, when everyone slept,
Sammy stood in the moonlight. He
felt a lovely glow inside. His friends
helped make his dream come true.
He *couldn't* be happier. He was a
Christmas snowman!